THE
BIG
DEAL

THE
BIG
DEAL

ALISON
CRAGIN
HERZIG

VIKING

VIKING
Published by the Penguin Group
Viking Penguin, a division of Penguin Books USA Inc.,
375 Hudson Street, New York, New York 10014, U.S.A.
Penguin Books Ltd, 27 Wrights Lane, London W8 5TZ, England
Penguin Books Australia Ltd, Ringwood, Victoria, Australia
Penguin Books Canada Ltd, 10 Alcorn Avenue, Toronto, Ontario, Canada M4V 3B2
Penguin Books (N.Z.) Ltd, 182–190 Wairau Road, Auckland 10, New Zealand

Penguin Books Ltd, Registered Offices: Harmondsworth, Middlesex, England

First published in 1992 by Viking Penguin, a division of Penguin Books USA Inc.

1 3 5 7 9 10 8 6 4 2

Library of Congress Cataloging-in-Publication Data
Herzig, Alison Cragin. The big deal / by Alison Cragin Herzig.   p.   cm.
Summary: Sam's parents agree to let him have a puppy if he
will take care of it, but as the puppy grows into an enormous
dog, Sam isn't certain that he can keep his end of the deal.
I S B N   0 - 6 7 0 - 8 4 2 5 1 - 6
[1. Dogs—Fiction.] I. Title.
PZ7.H432478Bi   1992   [Fic]—dc20
91-42255   CIP   AC

Printed in U.S.A.   Set in 13 point Caledonia

For
Football, M.F.

THE
BIG
DEAL

C H A P T E R

·ONE·

Please, Wally. Why can't you do what the other dogs do?" Sam Bates pleaded.

Wally wagged his tail. He didn't seem to care that Mrs. Cheever had tied his leash to the telephone pole again.

"Heel! Sit! Down!" Mrs. Cheever was still barking commands. "Now stay. Stay! Stay! Stay! Use your hand signal. Keep eye contact!"

Over by the bandstand in the middle of

Boonsville's town square, all the other owners crept backward away from their dogs.

Sam groaned and wrapped his arms around his knees. Wally never heeled for more than a few steps. He never lay down, unless Mrs. Cheever sat on him. He never stayed, even when Sam stared at him so hard his eyes felt like marbles. The only thing he had learned to do was sit. For about two seconds.

"All right, that's enough for today," Sam heard Mrs. Cheever say. "Call your dogs to come. Praise them. Pat them. No, no! Not like that. How would you like someone to bang you on the top of your head? Scratch behind their ears. Tell them they're good, good dogs."

"You're a bad dog, Wally," Sam whispered. "A really bad dog." Wally stopped trying to get away from his leash. He tried to hide his head in Sam's lap instead. His brown eyes peered up through a fringe of hair.

"Now they'll make me take you back to that farm," Sam told him. "Because you won't do what I tell you."

Wally's mouth turned crooked and drooped at the corners. Sam called it his Charlie Brown face. It was the same look he'd had when Sam first saw him.

That had been last Christmas Eve, the day his parents had finally agreed to let him have a dog. Sam remembered the FREE PUPPIES sign on the lawn of the old farmhouse. He remembered the warm smell of cows and the puppies playing in the hay in the corner of the barn.

Wally was the smallest one. He was the only one with white paws and a white spot between his eyes. He was the only one with a crooked Charlie Brown mouth.

"You sure you want him?" the farmer had asked. "He's the runt of the litter."

"I'm sure," Sam said. "I'm going to call him Wally."

"What kind of dog is he?" his mother wanted to know. She sounded doubtful.

The farmer shrugged. "A mutt, I guess."

"Will he get a lot bigger?"

"Not likely. Him being a runt and all."

"Well, Merry Christmas, Sam," his father said.

"But remember the deal," his mother added.

Sam knew the deal by heart. He had to feed the dog. He had to brush the dog. And he had to walk the dog, twice a day, every day. His father couldn't do it because he sold encyclopedias and was on the road a lot of the time. His mother couldn't do it because she was the assistant principal at Sam's school. She had to leave before he did in the morning and she came home later. Besides, Sam was the one who had begged and pleaded for a dog.

"I'll remember," he said. "Promise."

The next morning under the tree Sam had found a dog bed with a red cushion, a bowl with "DOG" written on it, and a lot of dog toys, like chew sticks and fake bones and a rubber pig that squeaked. It had been his best Christmas ever.

Sam glanced back at the bandstand. All the other dog owners had left, but Mrs. Cheever was marching across the grass toward him in her

lace-up boots. Wally jumped up and bounded to the end of his leash.

"Sit!" Sam told him. "Be good! Act like you're sorry!"

Sam tried smiling at Mrs. Cheever.

"Wally will be a *lot* better next time," he said.

But Mrs. Cheever didn't smile back.

CHAPTER
· TWO ·

Wally's a nice, smart dog," Mrs. Cheever said even before she reached them. "But I'm sorry, Sam. This isn't working."

"Yes it is," Sam said. "It has to."

"It's just that he's so big, Sam," Mrs. Cheever went on as if she hadn't heard. "And you're, well, so small. He doesn't take you seriously yet."

"But he will," Sam insisted. "I know he will."

"Maybe next year, when he's older and you've grown a bit."

"Please, Mrs. Cheever," Sam said. "Can't you give me one more chance? Please."

"Next year. Bring him back next year." Mrs. Cheever patted the top of Sam's head and walked away. Mrs. Cheever was right about one thing, Sam decided. Being patted on the head felt awful.

And she was right about the big and small part, too. He was the smallest kid in the whole fourth grade except for his friend Dunker Mulloy. Dunker was so short she had to stand on tiptoe to use the water fountain. But Wally had grown about a hundred times bigger since last Christmas. It was only November and his paws were the size of bagels.

But Mrs. Cheever was wrong about next year. There wouldn't be a next year for Wally. Not now. Not after Wally had gotten away from him again and made that hole in Dunker Mulloy's hedge.

That was when his mother had signed Sam

and Wally up for obedience school. "You're not walking Wally anymore," she said. "Wally's walking you. He's too big. He's as big as a baby buffalo."

"Perhaps his father was an Irish wolfhound," Sam's father said. "Did you know that Irish wolfhounds are the biggest—"

"Whatever. It doesn't matter. If obedience school doesn't work, Wally has to go."

"But Mom, I feed him and I brush him." Sam pleaded. "Couldn't we just fence in the backyard?"

"The backyard is too small," his father said.

"And he's already dug up half my flowerbeds," his mother added.

"But he's stopped growing. I know he has."

"Wally might be happier back in the country," his mother said. "Where there isn't a leash law. Where he can run free. And we can always get you another dog. A little one this time, more your size."

"I hate small dogs!"

"I don't think he wants another dog, dear," Sam's father said.

But his mother had only shaken her head.

What was he going to tell her now?

A horn beeped. The station wagon was coming toward him through the traffic on Boonsville's main street. Through the windshield Sam could see his mother waving.

He had to think of something.

The station wagon pulled up by the curb. Sam opened the rear door. Then he untied Wally's leash. "In, Wally!" he ordered, and pointed. Wally jumped into the backseat. Sam knew he would. Wally loved car rides.

Sam climbed in beside him. "Sit, Wally," he commanded. He used the hand signal. Wally sat. He always sat in the car. He liked to look out the window and pretend he was a person.

"Why, Sam, that's wonderful!" his mother said.

"Mrs. Cheever says he's a nice, smart dog," Sam said.

His mother smiled. "I'm so glad he's learning. Remind me to thank Mrs. Cheever next time."

"There won't be a next time. Mrs. Cheever

says Wally doesn't have to come back anymore this year."

"He doesn't? You mean he's graduated? We'll have to tell your father. Have a little party to celebrate."

"Okay," Sam said. But it wasn't okay. He didn't want a party. He wanted to get home and call Dunker. Dunker was smart. Maybe she could figure out how he was going to walk Wally tomorrow.

C H A P T E R
·THREE·

What's the big deal?" Dunker said. She sat in the middle of Sam's bed hugging her basketball. "My dad's not mad about the hedge anymore."

"But my mom is," Sam said. "Obedience school was Wally's last chance."

"Oh, brother." Dunker's blue eyes widened. "You're right. This is a definite emergency."

Dunker and her older brother, Weasel, lived next door. Her real name was Priscilla, but she made everybody call her Dunker because she planned to be a basketball player.

"So what am I going to do?" Sam swiped at the dark brown hair on Wally's rear end with the special wire brush his mother had given him. Wally lay on the floor with his head in his little red dog bed. The rest of him hung out.

"Can I brush him?" Dunker asked. "Just a little? Just his tail? It'll help me think."

"No." Sam liked brushing. "I told you. I have to do it."

"Then at least can I give him his Milk-Bone? Just this once. Okay?"

Sam shook his head. The Milk-Bones were fun. Sam threw them and Wally caught them in midair. "I have to feed him. It's part of the deal."

"You never let me do anything," Dunker said. "And we don't even get to walk to school together anymore."

"I can't. I have to walk Wally."

"That deal you made stinks."

"What stinks is being small," Sam said. "Why can't I look like George Doolittle?"

"Nobody looks like Doolittle. That's why kids call him Giraffe. He's the biggest nine-year-old in the history of the world."

"I guess he was born big," Sam said.

"Maybe we've grown." Dunker jumped off the bed. "You want to measure again?"

Every week since the summer Sam and Dunker had been measuring each other on Sam's closet door.

"We already measured. A few days ago."

"People grow in spurts, you know. That's what my dad says. But measure me first. I need to grow about two feet before basketball starts."

Sam stopped brushing. Dunker took off her sneakers and pressed herself against the door. Sam made a pencil mark where her curly red hair ended. The new line was right on top of the old one. "Four feet one inch and a quarter," he reported. "The same as before."

"Are you sure? I've got to grow or I'll never make the team."

"You'll make it. You're a great shooter."

"Only when no one's around," Dunker said.

"Miss Grazenbrand says I need extra practice with someone guarding me. And tryouts start in two weeks."

"Measure me," Sam said. "I've only got until tomorrow."

The yellow pencil scraped above his head. "Hey! Wait a minute." Dunker checked the tape. "Four feet three inches! I don't believe it. That's a whole half-inch more."

Sam turned to look at the new line. It was true.

"I'll bet it's a spurt," Dunker said. "Can you feel your bones stretching?"

Sam stared down at himself. He looked the same and he felt the same. "I guess. A little."

"Call Mrs. Cheever. Tell her you're growing."

"No, I'm not." Sam stuck out a foot. "I just remembered. I forgot to take off my new sneakers."

Dunker slowly erased the new line. "Maybe we'd better measure Wally. We've never done that before."

Wally jumped up. He barked and turned in circles and licked Sam's face. "Stop it," Sam told

him. "No more slobber kisses. This is serious."
He hauled at Wally's collar. Dunker pushed
from behind. They dragged him to the door.

"Two feet eleven inches," Dunker announced.
"I think. You're a ton taller than he is."

"But that's sitting down," Sam said. "What if
he was standing on his hind legs? He'd be six
feet probably."

Dunker sighed. "I guess we'd better weigh
him, too."

Wally was too big to fit on the bathroom scale.
"We'll have to do him in parts," Sam said.

Wally's front half weighed 27 pounds. His
back half weighed 45. Sam added the parts together. Math was his best subject. Then he got
on the scale.

"Oh, brother," Dunker said. "He weighs like
15 pounds more than you do."

"More like 18 pounds." Sam slumped into his
desk chair. "No wonder I can't hold him anymore."

"Sam, wash up," his mother called from
downstairs. "It's almost time for supper."

Dunker picked up her basketball. "I guess I'd

better go home. Practice my dribbling." Wally followed her to the door. "You can always borrow my gerbil," she added. "Anytime."

"I don't want a gerbil."

"I know." Dunker scratched the white spot between Wally's eyes. "I didn't want one either."

At supper Sam found a balloon tied to the back of his chair. His mother had cooked a steak. "The bone is for Wally," she said, "because he's such a smart dog."

For dessert there was a chocolate cake with "Congratulations Wally" writtten on top in white icing.

"Did you know that chocolate is bad for dogs?" Sam's father said. "It can give them heart trouble." He was always saying things like that. Sam figured he read all the encyclopedias before he sold them.

"The cake's for Sam," said his mother. "Chocolate's his favorite."

"It's really good," Sam said. But he wasn't hungry.

After supper the telephone rang. It was Dunker. "Had any walking ideas yet?" she asked.

"No."

"Weasel says to tell you he grew four whole inches in fifth grade. So all you have to do is hang on for a year."

"How?"

"Don't worry," Dunker said. "You'll think of something."

But Sam worried while he got into his pajamas. He worried while he brushed his teeth. He worried while he hung from the bar across his bathroom door to make himself longer.

After his mother and father kissed him good night, he lay in bed staring at the ceiling. In the dark he could hear Wally gnawing at his steak bone. "Wally," Sam said. Wally stopped chewing. Sam felt a cold nose sniff his face. Then he felt the bed sag as Wally climbed up. Sam didn't stop him.

Wally stretched out. He put his head on the pillow right next to Sam's. A warm tongue licked

Sam's face. Sam put an arm around him. Wally trusted him. Wally loved him, no matter what. He was even better than an older brother like Weasel. He was better than anything.

"I won't let them take you back," Sam whispered. "Promise."

CHAPTER
·FOUR·

Wally was always waiting right beside Sam's bed when he woke up. It was as if he could hear Sam's eyes open. But the next morning, Wally wasn't there. He wasn't anywhere in Sam's room.

Sam tore down the stairs in his pajamas.

"Wally!" he shouted. Maybe his parents had found out about obedience school and taken him back without telling.

Only his mother was in the kitchen. "I was just coming to wake you."

"Where's Dad? Where's Wally?"

His mother poured milk into a bowl of Cheerios and sliced bananas. "Your father left already. And Wally's busy with his steak bone. Now sit down and eat your breakfast, Sam. I have to get to school extra early. We're hosting a big teachers' conference this weekend."

Wally appeared in the doorway. There was a ring of what looked like dirt around his mouth. Sam hugged him anyway. Then he fed him a piece of banana. Wally was the only dog in the world who loved bananas.

"Wear a heavy sweater. It's freezing out." Sam's mother stuffed papers into her briefcase. "And don't forget to walk Wally."

At the word *walk* Wally's ears perked up. He did a little galumphing dance around Sam's chair. Then he pushed at Sam's knee with a big white paw.

"In a minute," Sam told him. But he dawdled over his cereal. Upstairs it took him a long time to find his good blue jeans. He retied the laces on his new sneakers twice.

"I'm off now, Sam," his mother called. "And Wally's waiting."

"I know," Sam muttered.

When he came downstairs again, the house was quiet. Wally stood by the front door with his leash in his mouth.

Sam zipped up his red parka. He couldn't put it off any longer. Maybe Wally would remember some of the obedience school stuff. Maybe he'd obey better when there were no other dogs around to play with. Maybe this time Wally wouldn't see any squirrels or stray cats.

Maybe. Sam took a deep breath. "Okay, let's go, Wally."

The beginning part was easy. Wally bounded out of the house, but he always stopped at the first tree. And the fire hydrant. And Dunker's mailbox.

Sam wound the leash around his hand. "Heel, Wally," he said.

Wally danced along beside him, sniffing the cold air. "Good dog, Wally. Good dog!"

Wally broke into a trot. "No. Heel. Heel!"

Sam jerked the leash the way Mrs. Cheever had showed him. But Wally's back legs churned ahead. He pulled Sam through a pile of dead leaves.

"Sit, Wally!" Sam shouted.

Wally sat. For a couple of seconds. Then he was off again. Sam hurried after him. Wally veered from one side of the sidewalk to the other. Then he dragged Sam past the house with the pink plastic flamingos on the lawn. The leash stretched even tighter. Sam hung on with both hands.

"Sit, Wally!" he yelled.

Wally sat. "Good dog," Sam said. "Good, good dog!"

It was working!

"Sit!" Sam ordered again in front of the house with the swimming pool in the backyard.

Wally sat. And jumped up. And towed Sam past the bus stop. And sat. And jumped up again.

Sam's arms began to ache from hanging onto the leash, but he didn't care. The walk was almost halfway over. At the far end of the street he could see the clock tower of his school. As soon as they reached the house with the bushes and the white gateposts and the big truck parked in the driveway, it would be time to turn around and go back.

Then he saw the squirrel, a few feet ahead. Right in the middle of the sidewalk, staring at them.

Wally stopped dead. His tail quivered.

"No, Wally. No! Sit! Sit!"

Wally leapt forward. Sam felt a tremendous jerk, as if his arms were being pulled out of their sockets, and then nothing. He stumbled and fell.

The squirrel streaked away down the sidewalk with Wally one jump behind, trailing his leash.

"Whoa! Stop! Wait!" Sam got up and raced after them. He pictured another hole in another hedge. He pictured the squirrel and Wally tearing up the steps of his school, skidding and scrambling through the hallways straight into his mother's office.

The squirrel swerved suddenly off the sidewalk and shot up the trunk of a tree. Wally tried to climb after it. When Sam caught up, Wally was still on his hind legs, barking. Sam lunged for the leash and, as quickly as he could, wrapped it around the tree. Then he sprawled in the leaves to catch his breath.

He was saved.

Wally finally stopped barking. He nudged Sam's face and pawed at his knee.

"Okay," Sam said. "In a minute." His heart was still thumping against his chest.

"Are you all right?" a woman's voice asked.

"I'm fine." Sam scrambled to his feet. "I was just walking my dog." The strange woman wore a pink-and-white coat and she was holding one end of a pink leash. At the other end was the weirdest animal Sam had ever seen.

"I'm walking mine, too," the lady said.

Her dog didn't look like a dog at all. It was tiny and totally bald and it was wearing a pink-and-white coat, too.

"Her name is Lucy," the lady said. "She's a Mexican hairless. I got her as a wedding present."

Sam wondered why she hadn't given it back. "Do you live around here?" he asked.

"I just moved in. You're the first person we've met. Isn't that right, Lucy?"

Lucy sniffed Wally's feet. Wally whined deep in his throat. His tail whanged against Sam's arm.

"Why, Lucy, I think you like that big dog," the lady went on.

Wally bent his head and snuffled at the little dog's nose. Then he hunched down and inched toward her on his belly, like he was trying to look small. His tail waved like mad. Hairless Lucy planted her weeny paws and yipped at him. She reminded Sam of the squeaky toy pig his parents had given Wally for Christmas.

"What's your dog's name?" the lady asked.

"Wally. But I have to take him home now."

Lucy rolled onto her back and let Wally sniff her bald stomach. "This is wonderful," the lady said. "Usually Lucy's scared of everything. She's never liked another dog before."

"Come on, Wally," Sam said.

"Can we walk with you?" the lady asked. "Lucy, you want to walk with nice Wally?"

Sam unwound the leash from the tree. He hung onto Wally's collar, too, just in case. But all Wally wanted to do was stay with Lucy.

"I'm getting married tomorrow," the lady said, "but Lucy's coming on our honeymoon, aren't you, Lucy? I'm lucky she's so small. She fits perfectly in my purse."

Lucy pranced around under Wally's nose. Wally crept along behind her, sniffing at her pink coat. His head was as big as Lucy's whole body.

"My dog had a toy pig once," Sam said. "But he ate it."

The lady laughed. "Oh, dear, I hope he doesn't eat Lucy. I love her more than almost anything."

"He won't," Sam said. "Wally's friendly."

"He has a beautiful, sweet face," the lady said.

"Well, this is where I live," Sam said.

"Say we'll see you again soon," the lady told Lucy. She smiled at Sam. "I'm so glad we met you. Now Lucy has her first dog friend."

"Good-bye," Sam said. He closed his front door and sagged against it. Thanks to dumb, hairless Lucy, he'd made it home safely. For now.

There wasn't time to think about later. He had to feed Wally his Milk-Bone, make sure his bowl was full of water, grab his book bag, and make it to school before he got marked late again.

CHAPTER
· FIVE ·

When Sam reached school, the fenced playground was empty. He pushed open the heavy
doors and took the stairs two at a time. Dunker
was standing by his locker.

"Where were you?" she called as soon as she
saw him. "The last bell just rang. Did something
happen with Wally?"

"He got away again," Sam said.

"Oh, brother! I knew it."

Sam slammed his locker door shut. He wished Dunker hadn't reminded him.

"Hey, Sam! Wait up," George Doolittle shouted after math class. He walked kind of funny, Sam realized suddenly. All hunched over. The way Wally had walked when he was with Lucy.

"How'd you do on the test?" Doolittle wanted to know.

"Okay," Sam said. "I mean, I got them all right."

"That's great!" Doolittle said. He sounded like he really meant it. "I got them all wrong! I wish I was smart, like you."

Even with his shoulders scrunched, Doolittle was as tall as Wally on his hind legs. Sam stared up at him. He wondered how it would feel to be that big.

In English the teacher handed back his composition, "Interesting Facts About Dogs." Sam's father had shown him how to look up stuff in the encyclopedia. "Dogs have tear glands to keep their eyes from drying out," Sam had written at the end. "But dogs can't cry. Monkeys can't cry either. Only people can cry. I'd probably cry if something happened to my dog, Wally."

The comment in red pencil above the title read, "This *is* interesting, Sam. Good work!"

Sam had never gotten an A+ in English before. He tucked the composition into the pocket of his binder. He couldn't wait to show it to his mother.

Dunker saved a place for him at lunch. Across the table Doolittle was slurping up a second helping of tuna casserole and lima beans. Wally slurped up his food, too, and always looked around for more. He'd outgrown the little dish with "DOG" on it. Now he ate out of a big metal pail.

Sam wondered whether eating a lot made someone grow. He decided to have second helpings next time they served pizza.

"Hey, Giraffe," Dunker said. "Would you play basketball with me after school? You know, guard me while I practice my shooting. All you have to do is jump up and down and wave your arms."

"Can't today." Doolittle's mouth was full. "Makeup math." He swallowed. "But I could do it after supper."

"It's too dark by then," Dunker said.

She asked Emma Lee Benson next. Emma Lee played baseball with the sixth-grade boys, but she wasn't stuck-up about it.

"Sure," Emma Lee said. "As soon as I have enough signatures on my petition to start a Little League team."

"When will that be?" Dunker asked.

"I hope soon," Emma Lee said. "Spring training starts in March."

"I'd practice with you," Sam said. "Except I have to walk Wally."

"I know," Dunker said.

After last period Sam dropped by the principal's office. His mother was in a meeting, but Miss Grazenbrand was manning the reception desk. "My! An A+," she said when Sam handed her his composition. "Way to go!"

"Can you make sure Mom gets it?" Sam asked.

"No sweat."

Sam hesitated. "And Miss Grazenbrand, about Dunker. Dunker Mulloy."

"Dunker?" For a moment Miss Grazenbrand looked blank. "Oh, yes. Priscilla. Weasel's little sister."

"Yeah. Dunker. She's great at basketball. I mean, she'd be terrific on the team."

"I'd like to put her on, I really would." Miss Grazenbrand leaned over the desk and looked down at him. "If only she weren't so small. Most of the other girls are fifth and sixth graders, you know. I'm afraid she's going to have trouble shooting over them."

"But she can learn."

"I'm sure she can. With practice," Miss Grazenbrand said. She straightened up. "But it might be better if she waited until next year."

Next year. Why was it always next year?

Outside, the playground was deserted, except for a few kids hanging out by the gate. And Dunker. She was all alone by the basketball hoop.

Sam heard the clock in the clock tower strike

four. He was late already. But maybe Wally could wait for a few minutes.

"Hey, Dunker! Want to play some ball?"

"You mean it?"

Sam jumped around in front of her. He waved his arms. "Come on. Shoot."

Dunker dribbled and shot. The ball missed. By a lot. She tried again. The ball bounced off the rim.

"That was close," Sam said.

He jumped a little lower and didn't wave his arms as hard. Dunker tried shooting over him. She tried dribbling around him. Finally the ball swished through the net.

"I've got to go now," Sam said. "But that last one was great."

"One out of ten is terrible," Dunker said. Her mouth scrunched up like she was going to cry. "Usually I make them all. But thanks anyway. Thanks a lot, Sam."

Sam decided not to tell her about Miss Grazenbrand. Besides, there wasn't time. But when he looked back he could still see her through the wire fence, dribbling and shooting.

CHAPTER
·SIX·

When Sam opened his front door, Wally came barreling to greet him. His whole body wagged and he whimpered with happiness.

"It's okay," Sam said. "I'm back."

"So am I," said his father.

"Dad? What are you doing home so early?"

"At the moment, I'm cleaning." His father held up a dustpan and broom. "Wally made a mess in the living room."

"Wally! How could you?" Wally stopped

jumping around. His mouth turned down. He flattened himself on the floor and tried to hide his face with his paws. "But it's not his fault, Dad. I'm late."

"Not that kind of a mess. Only dirt. He buried his steak bone in your mother's ficus tree. Besides, I walked him already."

"You did?"

"It was an interesting experience."

Sam stopped rubbing behind Wally's ears. He didn't like the way his father had said "interesting" and he didn't like the look on his father's face.

"Don't worry about the cleaning, Dad," Sam said quickly. "I'll do it. You rest."

"Tell you what. Why don't you make us some hot chocolate instead? Then we'll talk."

Sam didn't like the way his father said "talk" either.

In the kitchen he slowly spooned cocoa into two mugs. He poured milk into a pot and carefully put the carton back in the refrigerator. Wally trailed after him, sniffing at his hands.

"No chocolate," Sam said. He dumped dry

dog food into Wally's pail and added water to make gravy.

The milk in the pot bubbled. Behind him Sam could hear his father closing cupboard doors.

"No harm done," his father said. "Clean as a whistle."

Sam carried the mugs to the kitchen table. "Don't tell Mom, okay?"

"Okay. At least not about the ficus tree."

Sam kept his head down. He wished he could think of a way to escape to his room.

Wally nosed his pail across the floor trying to get at the last bits.

"Look at him, Dad. Isn't he cute?"

"Did you know," his father said, "that dogs are the only animals that can be trained without using food as a reward?"

"I got an A + on my composition about dogs," Sam said. He could feel his father's eyes staring at him.

"And did you know," his father went on, "that some obedience schools teach dogs to obey only their owners?"

"I guess."

"I was just wondering whether Mrs. Cheever taught Wally to obey only you."

Sam watched the swirls of foam in his cocoa. "Wally sits. Really well."

"That's a start," his father said. "But what happened to *heel*? And *slow down* and *whoa*?"

"It's not what you think," Sam said. "It's not Wally."

"Who is it, then?" his father asked.

"It's me," Sam burst out. "Wally could have learned all that, but I'm too small to control him. That's what Mrs. Cheever said. She said I had to grow. But I'm not growing. And it's all your and Mom's fault. I got the small genes from you. Not like Doolittle. I wish I had Doolittle's parents."

"You mean George? The one they call Giraffe?"

"Doolittle's so lucky!"

"I wonder if Doolittle thinks he's lucky," his father said.

"He's not a shrimp, like me," Sam said. "Other kids never pick him up and carry him around the way they used to do with me last year. Grown-ups don't have to bend over when they talk to him. And *his* parents aren't going to take his dog away."

His father got up and rinsed his cup in the sink. "Let me see your feet," he said.

"Why? What's wrong with them?"

"Aren't those new sneakers?"

"Mom had to buy them," Sam said. "The others got too tight."

"That's what I mean," his father said. "Did you know that the size of a person's feet is one way to tell how tall they're going to be when they're older? And your feet . . . well, check them out."

Sam peered under the table. The sneakers at the end of his skinny blue-jeaned legs looked as big as clown shoes. "You mean it, Dad?"

"I'm surprised you don't trip over them," his father said.

"Hey, Wally, did you hear that?" Wally lifted his head out of his empty pail. Sam jumped up. "I've got to call Dunker. I've got to start a foot chart!"

"Not so fast," Sam's father said. "We still have a big problem with Wally."

"But Dad . . . "

"No buts," Sam's father said. "Your mother is right. He's too much for you. He was almost too much for me. I'll walk him again tomorrow morning, but if you haven't thought of a solution by Sunday, I'll have to drive him back to the farm."

"Sunday! I can't grow by Sunday!"

"Then use your A + brain instead," his father said.

CHAPTER
·SEVEN·

When Sam woke up on Saturday morning, the first thing he saw was Wally's bright brown eyes staring back at him. A Post-it note was stuck to Wally's forehead.

"Wake up, sleepyhead," it read in his father's writing. "I've been out already. And fed."

Sam found two more notes on the refrigerator, both from his mother. "Homemade cranberry muffins in the wicker basket," and "Go to Dunker's if you get lonely. Your father's on the road, but you can reach me anytime at school."

Sam's A+ composition lay on the kitchen table tagged with another note. "This is terrific, Sam. And I know how you feel about Wally. I'd really cry if anything happened to you. Love, Mom." *Really* and *anything* and *you* were underlined twice.

The last note was from his father. It was pasted to Wally's leash. "THINK!" was all it said, in capital letters.

Sam thought while he ate a muffin. Then he brushed Wally and pitched two Milk-Bones for him to catch. After that he started a foot chart on the floor of his closet. He called Dunker to tell her, but her mother said she wasn't home.

At lunchtime he made himself a peanut butter and jelly sandwich. Then he remembered Doolittle and the tuna casserole and made himself another. He ate the middles and Wally ate the crusts in front of the TV. When the last of the cartoons were over, he and Wally played a wrestling game. Wally was Mad Dog Bates and Sam was the Superhuman Hunk.

"Okay, let me up," Sam said finally. He went

to check the clock in the kitchen. It was after two o'clock already. He tried phoning Dunker again, but she still wasn't back.

From the kitchen he could see Wally's leash, hanging from the knob of the front door.

Sam remembered the first time he'd taken Wally out. Wally had toddled along right by his feet, sniffing at the patches of leftover snow. He'd piddled sitting down and played with the leash and tried to walk between Sam's legs. Sam had showed him off to Dunker and Weasel. He'd wanted everyone to see him with his dog.

It was different now. Sam sighed. He went back to thinking.

Maybe he could make a trail of Milk-Bones on the sidewalk for Wally to follow. But then Wally would get even bigger and fatter.

Maybe he could borrow a whole football uniform, including a helmet. He'd be twice his normal size in all that stuff. But underneath he'd still be small. He still wouldn't be strong enough. And he'd look stupid. Like a little kid in a too-big snowsuit.

Maybe he could add a piece of rope to Wally's

leash and tie it to a tree. If the rope was long enough, that might count as a walk. Especially if his parents weren't home.

But it would have to be a really long rope.

Through the window Sam could see the afternoon sun shining through the bare branches of the trees. If only there were no squirrels. If only there was nothing for Wally to see.

And then he had it. A great idea!

"Hey, Wally. You want to go for a walk?"

Wally almost knocked him down with kisses. He galumphed into the hall and pulled his leash off the doorknob.

"Wait a minute," Sam said. "I just have to find something." He dragged a chair to the closet and climbed up. All the scarves were piled on the top shelf.

Sam decided the heavy wool kind might itch. He picked one of his mother's light, silky ones.

"Sit, Wally. Sit." Sam snapped on the leash. "Sit." He wrapped the scarf around Wally's head until his eyes were covered. Then he tied the ends behind Wally's ears.

Wally rubbed at the scarf with a paw and whined.

Sam zipped up his parka and opened the door. "It's okay, Wally. It's only a blindfold. Pretend it's night."

But Wally wouldn't move.

Maybe it was too dark under there. Maybe Wally needed to see a tiny bit. Sam fiddled with the scarf.

"Okay. Now come on. Let's go."

Wally stood up. He stumbled on the steps. Sam led him down the front walk. Wally sniffed at Sam's hands like he did when he wanted food.

"Later," Sam told him. "Milk-Bones later."

They started down Sam's road. Wally put one paw slowly in front of another. Walking was so easy, Sam almost laughed. Wait until he told his father. It was easier than when Wally was a puppy. Sam didn't even have to say "heel." Wally shuffled along right beside him without being told.

But he didn't stop at Dunker's mailbox like he usually did. And he didn't stop at any of his favorite trees.

Sam dragged him over to the fire hydrant. But Wally didn't seem to know what it was. He whined and tried to sit down.

"Don't worry." Sam tugged at the leash to get him going again. "I'm right here. Just follow me."

They passed the swimming-pool house.

"It's like a game, Wally," Sam said. "Pretend we're playing a game."

But Wally didn't seem to think it was a game. He kept pawing at the scarf. His mouth was totally crooked.

They crept past the bus stop.

In the distance Sam heard music, like someone was playing a stereo with the windows open. Wally's ears pricked up for a moment. Then they drooped again. He tucked his tail between his legs and dragged along.

"Please, Wally," Sam pleaded. "You'll get used to it. It's just until I grow."

The music grew louder. Cars lined both sides of the road. Beside the house where they'd met Lucy was a big green-and-white tent with clear plastic sides. Inside the tent Sam could see tables and chairs and a crowd of people.

"Look, Wally," Sam said. "Someone's having a party."

Wally pressed his head against Sam's leg. He licked Sam's hand. Then he lay down on the sidewalk and covered his face with his paws, like he did when he was a bad dog.

"No," Sam told him. "You're good." But Wally only whimpered and lay even flatter, like he'd given up.

Sam knelt down and rubbed the white spot between Wally's eyes. But Wally didn't move. He didn't even look like Wally anymore. He looked like someone's old fur rug.

Sam thought about his parents. He thought about the farm. After a while he checked the sidewalk and the nearest trees and as far back toward his house as he could. No squirrels.

"Okay, Wally," he whispered. "I'll figure out something else."

Then he untied the scarf.

CHAPTER
·EIGHT·

For a moment Wally scrubbed at his eyes as if he couldn't believe it. Then he was up in a flash, wagging and leaping and licking.

Sam hugged him. This was almost the best thing about Wally. Wally never blamed him for anything.

"You can have a whole piece of chocolate cake, promise," Sam said, "if you let me walk you home."

Wally barked and barked, as if this time he really understood.

Then Sam heard little answering yips. He looked over his shoulder. Lucy stood by one of the gateposts, dressed in a weeny white coat. White bows were tied around her pink, hairless ears.

Wally went all still. His tail quivered.

Lucy pranced closer. Sam stared at her. Maybe he could get her to come over. Maybe he could catch her and use her to help lead Wally home.

"Here, Lucy," he called. "Here, Lucy, you dumb dog."

Lucy stopped with one paw lifted. Then suddenly she turned and scampered back toward the tent.

"No, Wally! You stay!" Sam wrapped his arms around Wally's neck. He tried to block Wally's view with his body. "Stay!"

But Wally squirmed out of his grasp.

Sam chased after him, trailing the scarf.

Lucy streaked across the lawn with Wally right behind her.

Sam skidded to a stop at the opening to the tent. He saw Wally disappear between two tables. A woman in a yellow hat threw up her arms and screamed.

There were more yells and shouts. Table after table of people jumped to their feet, like people doing the wave at a ballgame. A lady in a white dress and a long white veil turned a surprised face toward him.

Sam ducked back out of sight.

"Watch out!" someone screamed.

"What is it? A mouse?"

Through the plastic side of the tent Sam saw a woman climb up on a chair.

"No. A bear!"

A man climbed up beside her. Two people carrying trays crashed into each other.

Sam dropped to the ground and peered under the plastic. Now all he could see were shoes.

"Catch it!" a man bellowed. "Tackle it!"

"The cake! The cake!"

"Save the cake!"

There was a huge crash. The music stopped. For a moment Sam froze where he was. Then he crawled backward away from the tent as fast as he could.

When he reached the gateposts, he huddled behind a bush. A man in a white bow tie came hurrying out of the tent and looked around. Finally the man went back inside.

Sam stayed where he was.

After a while he tried calling, "Wally, Wally," a few times, but he didn't dare yell. The people might hear him.

At least they had stopped screaming. At least nobody else had come running out of the tent. But this was worse than Dunker's hedge. It was worse than anything. The lady in the veil was Lucy's owner. And Wally had messed up her whole wedding.

Sam wondered if she had called the police.

Suddenly the band began to play again, and Sam heard a roar of voices. The people were singing a song about a doggie in a window.

Sam peered around the bush. He tried to make himself go back there. But he couldn't. Not all alone. It was too embarrassing. And even if he did, how would he ever make Wally come home with him?

There was only one thing left to do. Sam didn't want to do it. But he couldn't stay crouched behind the bush for the rest of his life. He had to go to school and find his mother.

CHAPTER
· NINE ·

Sam knew he should run, but he didn't. He felt as if Wally were already gone for good. He didn't even have the leash anymore. All he had left was his mother's scarf.

He balled the scarf up and stuffed it in his pocket.

The school parking lot was full of cars and the lights were on in all the classroom windows. Sam slowed down even more. He wondered which room his mother was in.

In the playground two kids were playing basketball. Dunker! He'd forgotten all about her. And Doolittle. Dunker was shooting and Doolittle was leaping around in front of her waving everything, even his legs. He looked so funny that for a moment Sam almost forgot about Wally.

Then he broke into a run.

"What's wrong?" Dunker asked as soon as he reached them.

"It's Wally," Sam said.

Doolittle was still throwing his arms and legs around. "Stop," Dunker told him. "I'm not shooting anymore."

"What's happening?" Doolittle asked.

"Wally wrecked someone's wedding!" Sam said.

"Why?" Dunker said. "How?"

Sam told them. "So I've got to go get him. Or else I'm going to have to tell Mom."

"Oh, brother," Dunker said. "Come on, Giraffe. We've got to help rescue Sam's dog."

When they reached the house with the

gateposts, Sam pointed at the tent. "He's in there."

Dunker shifted her basketball from hand to hand. Doolittle's mouth hung open.

"That's a lot of people," he said finally. His shoulders were hunched as high as his ears.

"What are you going to say?" Dunker asked.

"I'll think of something." Sam started across the lawn. "Please, guys."

Dunker tucked her basketball under her arm. "We're coming. Right, Giraffe?"

"Right," said Doolittle.

The noise from the tent grew louder and louder. Sam hesitated at the opening. The people at the tables were talking and laughing as if nothing had happened. Other people were dancing. At the far end of the tent the band was playing.

No one paid any attention to the three of them.

"Look at that cake," Dunker whispered into Sam's ear.

It was on a table near the bandstand. Sam had

never seen a cake that tall. But something was wrong with it. It was all tilted to one side, like it was melting.

"Do you see Wally?" Sam whispered back.

Dunker stood on tiptoe. She shook her head. "Maybe they've taken him to the pound."

"There's a big hairy dog lying right beside the drummer," Doolittle said suddenly. "With a little stuffed animal. I think it's a pig in a coat."

"That's him! That's Wally," Sam said.

"Maybe we can sneak around and get him without anyone noticing," Dunker said.

A couple of people at the nearest table glanced at them and smiled.

"Try to look small," Dunker hissed at Doolittle.

Doolittle doubled over.

"No. Act normal," Sam said. "Not like you're going to throw up."

Doolittle bent his knees instead.

They crept behind a long table covered with food. Sam saw Wally's tail first and then the rest of him. A big white bow was tied around his neck. And dumb Lucy was lying right between his front paws.

"Okay," Sam said. The drummer was beating away with his head back and his eyes half closed. "First we grab his leash. Then we drag him out through that opening in the corner."

"What corner?" Doolittle asked.

Dunker groaned.

"I'll count to three," Sam told them. "One, two . . ."

"That's him!" a voice shouted suddenly. The drummer's eyes snapped open. Sam saw Wally lift his head. "There he is!"

It was the bride. She came charging across the dance floor, pulling the man in the white bow tie along behind her. "Look, darling, that's the boy!"

Sam felt his stomach grow cold and his face get hot. Then Wally barreled into him, knocking him flat. He sat on Sam's chest and covered his face with kisses. Sam tried to roll free. Lucy yipped right next to his ear.

"Get off him, you big lug!" shouted Dunker.

Someone pulled Wally away.

Sam sat up. A circle of strange faces stared down at him.

"Watch out for that dog!" The woman in the yellow hat elbowed through the crowd. "He's going to run again!"

"We've got him," Doolittle said.

Sam climbed slowly to his feet. Dunker and Doolittle were hanging onto Wally's leash.

"Where were you?" the bride asked. She scooped Lucy up in her arms. "You missed all the fun."

"You call that fun?" the woman in the yellow hat wailed. "He almost bowled me over. He ruined the cake. He crashed into the drums."

"Now, Mother, don't start up again," the bride said. "You're going to scare him away."

"Scare *him?* His dog scared *everybody* half to death!"

"I'm really sorry," Sam said. "Really."

"Don't be sorry," the bride said. "It wasn't anywhere near that bad."

"But what about the cake?" Sam said. "And everything."

"It's got grass on it," the woman in the yellow hat cried.

"I know, Mother. But we picked most of it off," the bride said. She turned back to Sam. "And Lucy's had the best time playing with Wally. They're the cutest things together. We've got it all on videotape." She kissed Lucy's nose. "No one will ever forget my wedding now. Will they, Lucy? Will they, darling?"

The man in the bow tie grinned at Sam. "Pleased to meet you," he said. "That's a pretty amazing dog." He stuck out his hand.

Sam shook it. He felt a little dizzy.

"And who are your nice friends?" the bride asked.

"We're . . . uh . . . the dog walkers," Dunker said. "Right, Giraffe?"

"Right." Doolittle nodded and nodded as if his head were on a spring. "We walk dogs and stuff."

"We do all kinds of jobs," Dunker added.

"Do you wash cars?" the man in the bow tie asked. "Mine's got 'Just Married' written all over it."

"I washed windows once," Doolittle said.

"But we've got to take Wally home now," Sam said.

"That's a very good idea," said the woman in the yellow hat.

"Oh, dear," the bride said. "Lucy will be devastated. I think she's in love. Can you wait one more second? I want to get a picture of all of us together. Please, Mother, find the photographer."

Sam put an arm around Wally's neck. Flashbulbs popped in his face. The bride kissed him. The man in the bow tie clapped him on the back.

"Say good-bye, Lucy," the bride said. She waved one of Lucy's tiny, hairless legs.

"Come, Wally. Come," Sam said. Wally whined and looked back at Lucy. Dunker and Doolittle hauled at the leash.

Wally came.

The band struck up the doggie song again.

The music followed them out of the tent. Wally kept trying to turn around, but Dunker and Doolittle dragged him across the lawn. "Good-bye. Good-bye," the bride called after them. She was still waving Lucy's leg.

CHAPTER
·TEN·

I can walk him now," Sam said when they reached the gateposts.

Dunker and Doolittle handed him the leash.

Wally dug in his paws. He craned his head back toward the tent.

"No more tent," Sam said. But Wally wouldn't budge.

"Here." Dunker took hold of the leash again. "It works better with two people."

Wally gave up. He started down the sidewalk. Doolittle loped along beside them.

Wally stopped to investigate the bus stop. He checked out a nearby tree.

"This is fun," Dunker said.

"Just wait till he sees a squirrel," Sam told her.

"Like that one there?" Doolittle asked.

"Where?"

"Right there."

Wally's ears pricked up. "Sit!" Sam yelled. "Sit!"

Wally lunged forward. Sam and Dunker hauled on the leash. Wally's front legs pawed the air. Finally he just stood and barked. The squirrel scampered up a telephone pole.

"Hey," Sam said. "We did it!"

"Can I have another turn?" Doolittle asked. "I've never walked a dog before."

Dunker traded places with him.

When they reached the swimming-pool house, Wally tried to swerve into the driveway. But Sam and Doolittle wouldn't let him.

"Okay, it's my turn again," Dunker said when they reached her mailbox.

"But we're almost home," Sam said.

"Can't we walk him a little more?" Dunker asked. "You want to, Giraffe?"

"I guess it's okay," Sam said.

"You can carry my basketball," Dunker said.

Wally trotted past Dunker's hedge. He trotted past Sam's house. Sam kept waiting for something bad to happen, but every time Wally tried to speed up, Dunker and Doolittle pulled him in.

At the other end of the road, they turned Wally around.

"It's Sam's turn now," Dunker said.

"That's okay," Sam said. "I get to walk him a lot."

"I wish I did," said Doolittle.

"You want to walk him again sometime?" Sam asked after a moment.

"You mean it?" Doolittle said.

"What about me?" Dunker asked.

"I've been thinking," Sam said to her. He bounced the basketball on the sidewalk.

"Maybe we could be real dog walkers. Like you said."

"You mean earn money?"

"I was thinking more like walking Wally."

"Every day?" Dunker said. "For free?"

"I don't have any money," Sam said. "But maybe . . . maybe we could make a deal."

"This better be good," Dunker said. "The deal you made with your parents stank."

"What if I play ball with you after school? We could walk Wally to the playground first and tie him to the fence. Then I'd guard you. And after that, we could walk him home."

"But what about the mornings?" Dunker asked.

"If you walked him with me in the mornings, I'd let you brush him whenever you wanted. And feed him some of his Milk-Bones."

"But what if I make the basketball team? They practice in the gym every afternoon."

Sam fell silent. He hadn't thought of that.

Doolittle cleared his throat. "There's me," he said. "I mean, I'm terrible at basketball. Miss Grazenbrand's always after me, but I hate it.

And I'm terrible at math, too. But I could walk him with you. I mean, when Dunker's not around."

"Hey, great!" Sam said. "And then, well . . . if you want, I could help you with math."

"Would you? If I flunk, they might put me back in third grade. And I'm too tall for fourth grade already."

Doolittle was right, Sam thought. He was even too tall for the sixth grade.

Wally whined and tugged at his leash.

"Sit," Sam told him.

Wally sat, for a second.

"Sit," Dunker ordered.

"Sit!" boomed Doolittle. He sounded just like Mrs. Cheever.

Wally looked surprised. He sat.

"How did you do that?" Sam asked.

"I don't know," Doolittle said. "I guess my voice is louder than yours."

"You know something, Giraffe?" Sam said. "You could be really good at this dog stuff. I'll bet you could even help me train Wally, to heel and stay and everything."

"You think? Really?" Doolittle's shoulders straightened. "Sit!" he boomed at Wally again.

Wally was still sitting. Sam scratched the white spot between his eyes. "We could be sort of a club," he went on. "A dog walkers' club."

"I've never been in a club before," Doolittle said.

"It's an idea," Dunker said. "And maybe we could walk other dogs, too. Like that Lucy. On weekends."

"And when we've walked her, I could wash that man's car," Doolittle said.

"Other people might even pay us," Dunker said.

"We could do lots of jobs," Sam agreed. "After we've walked Wally."

"Okay," Dunker said. "It's a deal. You in, Giraffe?"

Doolittle nodded.

"You hear that, Wally?" Sam said. Wally looked hopeful. His tail thumped the sidewalk.

"There's just one thing," Doolittle said. "Do

you think it would be all right if you stopped calling me Giraffe? It's bad enough being as tall as one. And I don't like George either. But Doolittle's okay."

"Deal," Sam said. "Besides, you're nothing like a giraffe anyway."

"We'll have to buy another leash for Wally," Dunker added. "So we each get to hold our own."

A horn beeped. Sam looked across the road. It was his father in the station wagon.

"Here, Dunker. Take your ball," Sam said. "I want to show him."

Dunker led the way, dribbling her basketball. Sam and Doolittle held the leash. They walked Wally home.

Sam's father climbed out of the car. "Well, I'll be darned," he said. "This is a sight for sore eyes."

"We walked him," Sam said. "Everywhere. And we're going to train him, too. Gir—I mean, Doolittle is even better than Mrs. Cheever."

"I believe it," his father said. "The three of you look like you could do anything."

"You want us to wash your car?" Doolittle asked.

"Or rake your leaves?" Dunker added. "Your lawn looks terrible."

"And we do party entertainment. Like at weddings," Sam said. "But you won't have to pay us a lot. Because you're my dad."

"Why don't we all go inside first," his father said, "and have some chocolate cake? To celebrate."

"Wally, too," Sam added. "A tiny piece. Just this once. Okay, Wally?"

Wally barked and sniffed Sam's hands. His crooked Charlie Brown mouth straightened. It turned up at the corners until his bottom teeth showed.

"Look!" Sam said. "He's smiling."

"Dogs can't smile," Dunker said.

Sam rubbed the white spot between Wally's eyes. He hugged his big, hairy head. "Wally can."